Hello, Family Members,

Learning to read is one of the most important accomplishments of early childhood. **Hello Reader!** books are designed to help children become skilled readers who like to read. Beginning readers learn to read by remembering frequently used words like "the," "is," and "and"; by using phonics skills to decode new words; and by interpreting picture and text clues. These books provide both the stories children enjoy and the structure they need to read fluently and independently. Here are suggestions for helping your child *before*, *during*, and *after* reading:

Before

- Look at the cover and pictures and have your child predict what the story is about.
- Read the story to your child.
- Encourage your child to chime in with familiar words and phrases.
- Echo read with your child by reading a line first and having your child read it after you do.

During

- Have your child think about a word he or she does not recognize right away. Provide hints such as "Let's see if we know the sounds" and "Have we read other words like this one?"
- Encourage your child to use phonics skills to sound out new words.
- Provide the word for your child when more assistance is needed so that he or she does not struggle and the experience of reading with you is a positive one.
- Encourage your child to have fun by reading with a lot of expression . . . like an actor!

After

- Have your child keep lists of interesting and favorite words.
- Encourage your child to read the books over and over again. Have him or her read to brothers, sisters, grandparents, and even teddy bears. Repeated readings develop confidence in young readers.
- Talk about the stories. Ask and answer questions. Share ideas about the funniest and most interesting characters and events in the stories.

I do hope that you and your child enjoy this book.

—Francie Alexander
Reading Specialist,
Scholastic's Learning Ventures

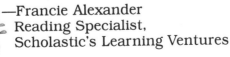

To my editor, Jordan
—K.M.

To Grace Croteau
—M.S.

Text copyright © 1999 by Kate McMullan.
Illustrations copyright © 1999 by Mavis Smith.
All rights reserved. Published by Scholastic Inc.
SCHOLASTIC, HELLO READER! and CARTWHEEL BOOKS and associated logos
are trademarks and/or registered trademarks of Scholastic Inc.

Library of Congress Cataloging-in-Publication Data
McMullan, Kate.
    Fluffy's 100th day of school / by Kate McMullan; illustrated by Mavis Smith.
        p.   cm. — (Hello reader! Level 3)
    "Cartwheel books."
    Summary: Fluffy the guinea pig enjoys himself when Ms. Day's class has a party
to celebrate the one hundredth day of school.
    ISBN 0-590-52309-0
    [1. Guinea pigs — Fiction. 2. Schools — Fiction.]   I. Smith, Mavis, ill.   II. Title.
III. Series.
    PZ7.M47879Fle   1999
    [E] — dc21
                                                                                    98-19109
                                                                                        CIP
                                                                                        AC
12 11 10 9 8 7 6 5 4 3   9/9 0/0 01 02 03 04

                            Printed in the U.S.A.   24
                            First printing, January 1999

FLUFFY'S
100TH DAY OF SCHOOL

by Kate McMullan
Illustrated by Mavis Smith

Hello Reader! — Level 3

SCHOLASTIC INC.
New York   Toronto   London   Auckland   Sydney

Fluffy's Pig Party

It was the 100th day of school.

Ms. Day's class had a party.

After the party, Wade asked,

"Does Fluffy know what day it is?"

"I don't think so," said Ms. Day.

Yes, I do, thought Fluffy.

It is today!

"Let's show Fluffy what 100 means," said Jasmine. "Let's have a '100th day of school' party for guinea pigs." And so they did.

Duke came to the party.
So did Kiss.
Lucky Sue came
from the kindergarten.
The kids put all the pigs
into Fluffy's play yard.

Fluffy had never
had a party before.
Uh...hi, he said to the other pigs.
Howdy, said Duke.
I'm a crested pig, said Kiss.
Oh, I just love parties! said Lucky Sue.
Fluffy was not sure
if he liked parties at all.

Emma counted out
100 sunflower seeds.
Maxwell put the 100 seeds
into a bowl in the play yard.
"Party on, pigs!" he said.
The pigs ran over to the bowl.
Wade and Jasmine started counting
how many seeds each pig ate.

Kiss stopped eating.

Let's rock in the coconut shell,
she said.

Oh, I just love to rock!
said Lucky Sue.

What are we waiting for? said Duke.

The pigs ran over to the shell.

Kiss, Duke, and Lucky Sue jumped in.

But there was no room for Fluffy.

He watched the other pigs rock.

He kept eating sunflower seeds.

Yahoo! yelled Lucky Sue. **What fun!**

Fluffy was not having fun.

He ate more sunflower seeds.

Duke started rocking harder.

Lucky Sue rocked like a wild pig.

Kiss rocked so hard that her crest

whipped around on her head.

CRACK! The shell broke.

What a cheap coconut, said Kiss.

I feel like chewing something up,
said Duke.

Oh, I love to chew things up!
said Lucky Sue.

Let's chew up that tube over there,
said Kiss.

No! said Fluffy.

Not my tube!

The pigs ran over to Fluffy's tube.
They started chewing it.
Fluffy nibbled more sunflower seeds
and watched the other pigs chew
his tube to bits.
He did NOT like parties.

"Fluffy just ate the last seed,"
said Jasmine.
She and Wade counted their tally marks.
"Duke ate 10 seeds," Jasmine said.
"Kiss ate 15," said Wade.
"Lucky Sue ate 25.
How many did Fluffy eat?"
"I'm not sure," Jasmine said.
"He ate so fast,
it was hard to count."

Wade added up the seeds
the other pigs had eaten.
"They ate 50 seeds in all," he said.
"Fluffy ate the rest."
"Then Fluffy ate 50 seeds!" said Emma.
"That's half a hundred!"

"The winner of the seed-eating contest
is Fluffy!" said Wade.

"Hooray for Fluffy!" all the kids cheered.

No fair! Kiss told Fluffy.

I didn't know it was a contest!

I didn't know either, said Fluffy.

He burped.

Maybe he liked parties after all.

Fluffy's Big Race

Emma and Jasmine made a race track
100 inches long.
They put the guinea pigs
on the starting line.
I am going to win this race,
said Kiss.
Lucky Sue said, **I love to run!**
Duke smiled. **They don't call me
Speedy Duke for nothing,** he said.
Fluffy burped again.

"On your mark," said Emma.

"Get set. Go!"

The pigs were off!

Duke took the lead.
Kiss and Lucky Sue
were right behind him.
Fluffy tried to catch up.
But he could not go fast.
His tummy was too full
of sunflower seeds.
"Go, Fluffy!" called Emma.

Speedy Duke was really moving.

But then he stopped.

He sniffed.

There were some crumbs on the floor
from the party.

Duke dashed over to the crumbs.

"Duke is out of the race," said Jasmine.

Lucky Sue took the lead.
I love running! she said.
It makes me so happy,
I feel like twirling!
She did a little spin.
Then Lucky Sue
started running again.

"Uh-oh," said Maxwell.
"Lucky Sue is running
the wrong way."
Lucky Sue ran across
the starting line.
I love winning! she said.
"Lucky Sue is out of the race,"
said Maxwell.

Only Fluffy and Kiss were left.
Kiss looked over her shoulder
at Fluffy.
Give up! she told him.
Never! said Fluffy.
He was huffing and puffing.
He promised himself never to eat
50 sunflower seeds again.

Kiss kept looking
over her shoulder.
She was not watching
where she was going.
All of a sudden, she tripped.
Her feet slipped out
from under her.
Ooof! she said as she fell.

"Poor Kiss!" cried Emma.

She quickly picked Kiss up.

Kiss kicked her feet in the air.

Fluffy heard Kiss squealing:

Let go! Put me down!

I have to win this race!

But Emma put Kiss in her lap.

She petted her fur.

"You'll be okay, Kiss," said Emma.

Fluffy kept going all by himself.

At last he crossed the finish line.

"Fluffy ran 100 inches!" said Maxwell.

"Fluffy wins the race!" said Wade.

Fluffy smiled.

They don't call me Fast Fluffy for nothing, he thought.

The Mystery

Ms. Day's kids took
Kiss, Duke, and Lucky Sue
back to their classrooms.
They put Fluffy in his play yard.
Then they went out for recess.
Fluffy's cardboard box
had been turned upside down.
He crawled on top of his box.

He thought about the race,
and how good it felt
to be Fast Fluffy.
A bowl of cherries
was on the counter
next to the play yard.
Big dark red cherries.
They look yummy,
thought Fluffy.
He was starting to feel hungry
again after his big race.

The kids came in from recess.
Ms. Day picked up the bowl.
She said, "Guess how many cherries
Jasmine and Wade put in this bowl?"
"One hundred!" everyone said.
"That's right," said Ms. Day.
"We are going to have them
for a snack. How many people
do we have in this class?"

"There are eighteen kids,"
said Jasmine.
"And one teacher," said Wade.
"That makes nineteen," said Emma.
"And Fluffy makes twenty,"
said Maxwell.
Count me in!
thought Fluffy.

Ms. Day gave Maxwell and Emma
twenty paper cups.
"Please put the cherries
in the cups," she said.
"Each cup will have the same number
of cherries in it."

Emma put one cherry in each cup.

Maxwell put a second cherry in each cup.

Emma put a third cherry in each cup.

Maxwell put a fourth cherry in each cup.

Emma put a fifth cherry in each cup.

But there was no fifth cherry
for the last cup.

"Ms. Day!" Maxwell called.

"The last cup only has four cherries.
There were only 99 cherries
in the bowl."

"We put in 100 cherries," said Jasmine.

"Maybe you counted wrong," said Emma.

"No way," said Wade.

"We counted exactly 100 cherries."

"This is a mystery," said Ms. Day.

Jasmine took the last cup over to Fluffy.
She dumped the four cherries
into his food bowl.
"Four cherries are enough
for you, Fluffy," Jasmine said.
Fluffy jumped off his food box and ran over
to his food bowl.

"Ms. Day!" Jasmine called.
"The mystery is solved."
Everyone ran over
to Fluffy's play yard.
"Look what I found
on top of Fluffy's box," she said.

And she held up a cherry pit.
"My goodness!" said Ms. Day.
"How did Fluffy ever get a cherry?"

Heh heh, thought Fluffy.

**They don't call me Clever Fluffy
for nothing.**